FRAGMENTS TO WHOLENESS

A JOURNEY BACK TO SELF

SYLVIA TORRES VILLALOBOS

COPYRIGHT 2025 FRAGMENT to WHOLENESS

by Sylvia Torres Vllalobos

ISBN

Hardbound-978-621-495-384-4

Softbound/Paperback-978-621-495-385-1

PDF (read only)-978-621-495-386-8

Published by:
Poetry Planet Book Publishing House
Rosario, Pozorrubio, Pangasinan, Philippines
Contact Number:075-6155455
Email: maritesritumalta@gmail.com

Author's Preface

In many ways, this book is not just a collection of words—it is a mirror of my soul, a mosaic of the broken pieces I have gathered over the years and painstakingly pieced back together. "Fragments to Wholeness: A Journey Back to Self" is deeply personal and universally relatable. It is the story of unraveling, falling apart, and finding a way to become whole again.

When I began this journey, I was unaware of how fragmented my life had become. I was carrying wounds that I had buried so deeply, that I forgot they existed. Like many of us, I wore a mask of strength, convinced that ignoring my pain was the same as healing from it. But as the days turned into years, the weight of that unaddressed pain became unbearable, and the cracks in my carefully constructed facade began to show.

This book was born from the healing process that followed. Writing became my sanctuary, a place where I could explore the depths of my emotions and examine the pieces of my life that no longer fit. It was here that I discovered the power of vulnerability, the courage it takes to face oneself, and the profound transformation that comes when we stop running from our pain and instead choose to embrace it.

"Fragments to Wholeness" is not a how-to guide or a list of steps to fix a broken life. Instead, it is an invitation to reflect, to feel, and to connect with your own story. It is a journey through grief and joy, despair and hope, loss and rediscovery. It is about finding beauty in imperfection and strength in our struggles.

As you turn these pages, I hope that you will find pieces of yourself in my story. That you will see your own strength mirrored in the words and recognize the resilience you carry within. Healing is not linear, and it is not easy. But it is possible. And it is worth it.

Thank you for allowing me to share my journey with you. My hope is that it serves as a gentle reminder that, no matter how broken we may feel, wholeness is always within reach.

With love and gratitude,

The Author

1

If someone decides to walk away from you because you've tried to have a conversation about how you feel because of the way they're treating you, neglecting you, or disrespecting you; they were never interested in being respectful towards you anyway.

Not only that, but they were gas lighting you into believing that they actually cared about you, or that they even loved you. Because someone who loves you doesn't just walk away after they've hurt you.

If you've had to say the same thing to someone time and time again, and you have to keep explaining to them how it upsets you time and time again; that's not a misunderstanding, that's disrespect!

People who truly love you hurt when you hurt!

People who love you don't keep doing the same thing over and over again knowing that it upsets you, or that it hurts you in some way.

Don't be afraid of losing people who want to make a habit of being disrespectful towards you, or are okay with knowing that they're hurting you. And don't ever think you did the wrong thing or that you made a mistake by asking to be treated with decency and respect.

The problem wasn't that you wanted to discuss their disrespect with them, the problem was the fact that they weren't even willing to discuss it or show any empathy or compassion towards the way they've made you feel...

Know your worth, let them go, and know that you deserve better.

2

Make the change. This is one of the hardest things you will ever have to do in your lifetime and it will also be one of the most important. Stop having in depth conversations with people who don't see a problem in their actions. Stop being there for people who have no interest in your presence.

When you begin to fight for a life with happiness, passion and commitment, not everyone will be ready to follow you to this particular place. This doesn't mean you need to change who you are, it just means you should let go of the people who aren't ready to accompany you. If you are forgotten or ignored by the people who you give your time to, you do yourself a favor by not continuing to offer your energy and your time to these particular people.

The truth is... that you are not for everyone, and not everyone is for you. That's what makes it so extraordinarily special when you meet someone who can reciprocate the love you give to them. The more time you spend trying to make someone love you, the more time you waste depriving yourself of the possibility of this connection to someone else. The more you stay involved with someone who uses you as a pillow, or a therapist for emotional healing, the longer you stay away from the person you long for.

Maybe... if you stop showing up, you won't be wanted. Maybe... if you stop trying, the relationship will subside. Maybe... if you stop texting them, your phone will stay silent for days. That doesn't mean you ruined the relationship, it means the only thing holding it back was the energy that only you gave to keep it. This is not love, it's an attachment.

You deserve so much more than what you are settling for. The most valuable thing you have in your life is your time, and it's very limited. When you give your time to someone that is something you can never get back so choose wisely who you decide to spend it on. Make your life a safe haven, in which only compatible souls are allowed.

You are not responsible for saving anyone. You are not responsible for convincing them to improve. It's not your job to exist for people and give your life to them. Take my advice and make a change that will give you the protection, happiness and the love you truly deserve.

3

The only way to get the best of an argument is to avoid it. Silence is one of the hardest arguments to refute.

4

People who feel everything so deeply can never turn off our
hearts.
We want the world and everything in it.
We want to hold it tightly, we want to keep it close by; we don't
want to lose it.
We feel obligated to save people, to fix things, to make it better.
We need to feel loved and give love as well.
Our hearts beat for, and because of, all of the people we have
the potential to care for.

We're are the eager ones. And yes, we feel too much.
I wish I had answers as to why we were chosen to be the fragile
ones,
the easy-to-crumble ones, the heavy-hearted ones.
I wish I knew why we are the ones who carry all of our
emotions in our back pockets.

I wish I knew why all of the easy stuff is so hard for us.
Why when it's all said and done we still feel hurt by a world that
isn't listening, that isn't the same as us.
But I'd like to think that one day the strength and love we try to
give to the world will be appreciated.
That caring deeply for others will pay off.
Because truthfully, we are rare and beautiful souls.
We are needed to make this world a little less heavy.

So wherever you are, whoever you are,
if you feel things deeply please don't stop being you.
Please don't stop loving the world and everyone who comes
into yours.

Please don't stop hoping for better days;
don't stop trying to get it right, to make things good.
Soon enough you will run across someone
who will see all these things in you and call them beautiful.
They will be glad to have met you.
They will fill that empty place.
They will call you home.
You dear, have a heart of gold.
Don't let the world diminish that.

5

A mistake is something done by accident, something that is not planned. But cheating and lying are not mistakes; they are known choices. When someone cheats or lies, they have decided to break the trust and hurt the other. It's not accidental; it is intentional. Mistakes can be pardoned because they are done without any intention, but cheating and lying depict lack of respect and honesty. If you really care for a person, you don't make decisions that will hurt them. Love is built on trust, and such intentional actions can destroy it. Choose honesty and loyalty always.

6

Never defend yourself to a narcissist.

They thrive on watching you spin your wheels, trying to prove a truth they'll never accept. Whether they know you're right or not doesn't matter—what they want is control, and your frustration feeds it. They love to pick fights. They'll bait you, provoke you, and push every button, all for the thrill of seeing you react. Don't give them the satisfaction. Reclaim your peace and walk away from their games. The best power move? Stay grounded in your truth and refuse to engage.

7

He who lives naively trusting dies abused, misused, and betrayed. Life demands a balance between trust and awareness. Blindly trusting without listening to the whispers of your instincts leaves you vulnerable to those who may exploit your kindness or take advantage of your open heart.

Trust is beautiful, but trust without discernment is dangerous. Your instincts are there for a reason—they are the quiet protectors of your soul, the voice inside that senses what words cannot reveal. Ignoring them is like walking through a storm with no shelter, hoping the rain won't touch you.

But life doesn't work that way. People, situations, and intentions can sometimes hide behind masks, and your intuition is your guide through the maze of it all. To live wisely is not to stop trusting but to trust with open eyes and a steady heart. It's understanding that while there is goodness in the world, there are also lessons to be learned, and not every hand extended to you is offering help.

By honoring your instincts, you protect your boundaries, your energy, and your peace. When you blindly ignore the warnings within, you invite pain that could have been avoided. Abuse, betrayal, and misuse thrive in spaces where self-awareness is absent. But when you learn to trust yourself—when you sharpen your instincts and allow them to lead—you live with strength, resilience, and clarity.

Trust, but trust wisely. Believe, but never at the expense of your inner voice. The strongest person is not the one who trusts blindly but the one who trusts with understanding, with boundaries, and with a deep connection to their intuition.

8

They will entangle you into their web of deceit and manipulation. They'll speak of forever, of always, of never letting you go - but their words are as empty as their soul. They'll promise to be your rock, your haven, your forever home - but they'll prove to be a stormy sea, a raging fire, a devastating earthquake. They'll shatter your dreams, crush your heart, and leave you to pick up the pieces of your shattered life.

Their words are a poison, a venom that seeps into your veins, making you believe in a future that never existed. They're a master of make-believe, a weaver of false hopes, a siren luring you to the rocky shores of heartbreak. But still, we believe. We want to believe. We need to believe. Because the alternative is too terrifying to contemplate - that we've been duped, deceived, and manipulated by a person who never intended to keep their promises.

So we cling to the words, even as the actions betray them. We cling to the hope, even as reality destroys it. We cling to the love, even as it turns to dust in our hands. But eventually, we must face the truth. The narcissist's words are lies, their promises empty, their love a myth. And we must walk away, no matter how hard it is, no matter how much it hurts.

Because in the end, that's the only way to find true love - by letting go of the false. A narcissist is a person of many words initially. But never a person of their word. They will paint the future you've always dreamed of but deliver a nightmare you must recover from. That's not love. It's the opposite of love. It's a cleverly crafted illusion, designed to lure.

9

You didn't lose the love of your life; you broke free from the chains of a predator who drained your joy, strength, and identity. A narcissist isn't your soul mate—they're a master manipulator hiding behind a carefully crafted mask. The person you see at the end of the relationship, the one who discarded you without empathy, is who they've been all along. Their charm, their "magic," their love-bombing—all of it was a performance.

False promises and shallow words disguised their real agenda: to control, exploit, and feed off your emotional energy while breaking down your confidence. What you endured wasn't love —it was a calculated game of power. Gas lighting, criticism, and emotional manipulation weren't acts of affection but weapons used to keep you doubting yourself.

Their betrayals weren't mistakes; they were deliberate moves to hold you captive in their cycle of abuse. But here's the powerful truth: You didn't lose a family member—you escaped a nightmare. Walking away from that toxic cycle took unimaginable strength. Breaking free from someone who pretends to love but thrives on control isn't easy, but you did it. And now, you're standing in the light of freedom, no longer bound to their lies.

Healing begins when you accept this: you weren't loved, you were used. But that does not define your worth or your future. You were created for real love, genuine connection, and a life filled with joy, authenticity, and peace. You are worthy of being truly seen, deeply heard, and genuinely valued. Never settle for less than the love and respect you deserve. Real love isn't a game or manipulation—it's kind, patient, and true.

As you heal, remember this: the best is yet to come. You've reclaimed your life, and the right people, the right love, and the right future are waiting for you.

10

Dear Me,

Someday, you'll thank yourself for choosing to love yourself instead of settling for less than what you deserve. You will figure out one day that the pain that you feel right now is just a part of healing. You will never be in pain forever. You will realize that you made the right decision to walk away from people and places where you feel like you are unappreciated and unvalued. You are brave enough to choose yourself this time. You are brave enough to let go of all the things that hurt you, even though you love them more than anything else.

My dearest self, you are strong enough to survive all the suffering that you've been through, and I know that you'll be proud of it someday. I want you to know that you deserve to give yourself a break from everything that tortures your heart and soul. You deserve to be happy, even after any heartbreak. You deserve to give yourself peace, even after being miserable for so long. One day, you will thank yourself for treating yourself better than how other people treat you. And maybe that day, just like everyone else, you will finally understand that everything happens for a reason.

11

A deep woman often seeks qualities in a partner that go beyond the superficial, valuing depth, understanding, and connection. Here are some qualities she might look for in a partner:

1. Emotional Intelligence: She values someone aware of their own emotions and can understand hers. Emotional intelligence fosters empathy and helps in understanding her complex thoughts and feelings.

2. Authenticity: She's drawn to someone who is genuine and doesn't put on a facade. A deep woman wants her partner to show their true self, embracing flaws and imperfections.

3. Intellectual Curiosity: A deep woman often enjoys exploring new ideas and learning. She desires a partner who is curious, open- minded, and willing to engage in thoughtful conversations.

4. Emotional Availability: Emotional depth requires a partner who is open to connection and vulnerable enough to share their feelings and experiences.

5. Integrity and Honesty: She needs someone who is honest and keeps their word. This builds trust, which is foundational for her in a meaningful relationship.

6. Respect and Independence: She values respect in a relationship and wants a partner who encourages her independence. A deep woman appreciates a partner who respects her space, interests, and individuality.

7. Supportive and Compassionate: She seeks someone who will

support her dreams, ambitions, and emotional needs, offering encouragement through good and tough times alike.

8. Growth Mindset: A deep woman values a partner who seeks personal growth and encourages her growth too. Whether it's personal goals or relationship goals, she wants someone invested in evolving together.

9. Good Communicator: Open, honest, and respectful communication is essential for her. She looks for someone who is willing to talk about issues, listen actively, and resolve conflicts constructively.

10. Shared Values: Whether it's values on family, career, or personal integrity, a deep woman looks for alignment on the core beliefs that matter most to her. A deep woman desires a partner who can meet her in the richness of her emotional world, fostering a relationship built on authenticity, understanding, and mutual.

12

I'm going to be honest with you. It's not easy to forget about someone you truly love, someone who has become an integral part of your life, someone you have invested so much on, someone you are mentally and emotionally attached to, someone you have shared the best and most beautiful memories with, someone you understandings and felt like the person also does same. Honestly, it's not easy to let go of such a person.

No matter how easy I make "the move on" sound to you here,

it's never easy, and I understand, but the thing is that you have no option but to learn how to adapt in their absence. You see if you fail to gather the courage and strength to move on from a failed relationship, you will eventually keep hurting yourself, endangering your future, and destroying yourself in the present.

Life goes on. Feel bad as you want, but understand that when people are no longer interested in you anymore, there is nothing you can do about it. You can't control how people feel about you and their decisions, you must understand. If they are no longer for you anymore, it's their choice, and you can't do anything about it other than focusing on controlling what you can't, which is trying your best to find peace and move on.

Learn to accept reality. If you are the reason for the fallout and you have apologized and your apology fell on deaf ears, don't hurt yourself the more for the mistakes. Accept it and move on in good faith. You have to develop that strength to continue living even after so many disappointments. That's what life is all about.

Your ability to refuse to remain beaten is what success is all about. Move on, accept the memories you shared with the person, don't fight it. Think about those lovely moments and be happy you once had a life like that, then focus on building something like that in the future. Everyone is replaceable, believe me.

13

Narcissists don't date losers, they are losers, they choose people who are better than them and then do everything they can to bring them down because deep down, they're insecure, inadequate, and fearful of being exposed as the frauds they are. they're attracted to people who are confident, successful, and charismatic because they want to feed off their energy, their accomplishments, and their reputation, they want to bask in the reflected glory of someone else's success, because they're unable to achieve it on their own. but once they've got you in their sights.

They'll do everything they can to tear you down, belittle your achievements, undermine your confidence, and make you feel small, insignificant, and unworthy, because that's how they feel about themselves, and they can't bear the thought of someone else being better than them. so, if you're in a relationship with a narcissist, don't be fooled by their charm, their charisma, and their false promises, because beneath the surface, they're seething with insecurity, jealousy, and resentment, and they'll stop at nothing to destroy you, to control you, and to make you their puppet. remember, you deserve better than that, you deserve to be loved, respected, and valued for who you are, and you deserve to be in a relationship that lifts you, rather than tearing you down.

14

When someone is prepared to walk away from you, without any genuine apology for hurting you; you no longer owe this person anything! You don't have to give them anything more other than your silence. Because your silence is all they deserve. Your silence is your response to their lack of respect, their lack of empathy, and their lack of accountability for what they've done. By choosing to offer them nothing more than your silence, you are protecting your emotional well-being and your mental health. You are also sending a very clear message that you deserve to be treated with respect and kindness, and that you're not prepared to put up with their disrespect and lack of kindness towards you! Your silence doesn't mean they've won, it means you're now choosing peace over their chaos, drama, and disrespect.

15

Silent Sacrifices Of Her Heart She was the girl who smiled through her pain because she didn't want to burden you with her sadness. She was the girl who stayed up all night, fighting her own battles, just so she could be your strength the next morning. She was the girl who swallowed her pride every time you hurt her, just so she could keep the bond alive. When the world turned its back on you, she stayed, even when her own world was falling apart. She was the girl who begged in silence for your attention, while you were too busy noticing others. She was the girl who saw the best in you, even when you showed her the worst. And in the end, after giving everything she had, she left quietly, not because she stopped loving you, but because she realized you never truly loved her back.

16

Simple rule in life: if you wouldn't like it done to you, don't do it to others. This profound philosophy serves as a guiding light, illuminating the path to empathy, compassion, and kindness, and reminding us that the way we treat others is a reflection of our character, our values, and our humanity. By embracing this principle, we can create a world where everyone feels valued, respected, and loved, a world where kindness, empathy, and compassion are the guiding principles of our interactions with others, and where we can all thrive and reach our full potential.

As we navigate the complexities of life, let us remember that this simple yet powerful rule has the potential to transform our relationships, our communities, and our world never disrespect that person who made sure you were okay when nobody else did, because they were there for you when it mattered most, when you were at your lowest, when you were feeling lost and alone, and when you needed someone to care, to listen, and to support you, and they showed up, they stepped up, and they made a difference in your life,

A difference that you'll never forget, a difference that you'll always cherish, and a difference that you'll always be grateful for those people are rare, they're precious, and they're to be treasured because they're the ones who see the best in you, even when you can't see it yourself, they're the ones who believe in you, even when you've lost faith in yourself, and they're the ones who'll be there for you, no matter what, no matter where, and no matter when. so, never take them for granted, never disrespect them, and never forget what they've done for you, because they're the ones who've made a real difference in your life, a difference that's worth acknowledging, worth appreciating, and worth celebrating, and they're the ones who deserve your respect, your gratitude, and your love.

17

The end game of a relationship with a narcissist: After a while, you start not to care about the narcissist. The constant drama, the endless manipulation, the exhausting games - it all becomes too much to bear. You reach a point where you're numb to their antics, indifferent to their needs and unresponsive to their provocations. The spell is broken, and you see them for what they truly are: a master manipulator, a skilled deceiver, and a heartless exploiter.

You realize that their behavior is not about you, but about their insecurities, their fears, and their own desperate need for control. You start to detach, to let go of the emotional investment you once had in the relationship. You stop trying to fix them, stop trying to please them, and stop trying to understand them. You accept that they are who they are and that they will never change. With detachment comes freedom. You're no longer held hostage by their whims, no longer trapped in their web of deceit.

You're free to live your life, to pursue your own interests, and to cultivate meaningful relationships with others. You start to care about yourself, to prioritize your own needs, and to nurture your own well-being. You rediscover your own identity, your own values, and your own sense of purpose. You emerge from the toxic fog of the narcissist's world, blinking in the bright light of your liberation.

And when the narcissist tries to reel you back in, to manipulate you once more, you're immune. You see through their tactics, you resist their charms, and you maintain your distance. You know that you deserve better, that you're worth more, and that you'll never again surrender to their toxic grasp.

18

You cannot rescue anyone from their struggles. What you can do is be a steady presence, a calm anchor in their storm, and a source of unconditional support. You can offer your love, your understanding, and the wisdom you've gained from your own experiences. But their battles are their own to fight, their wounds are their own to heal, and their growth is theirs to achieve. No matter how deeply you care, you cannot carry their pain for them or force their healing process. What you can do is hold space for them—a space where they feel safe to express their fears and vulnerabilities without judgment. Your groundedness can remind them that peace and strength are possible, even in the midst of turmoil.

Your patience and kindness can help them feel less alone as they navigate their challenges. But their transformation must come from within. To take that from them would deny them the lessons, resilience, and clarity that come with facing their path. Supporting someone through their pain doesn't mean fixing their problems or taking control of their journey. It means respecting their process, even when it's painful or slow. It means letting them make their own choices, even when you might disagree. It means trusting that they have the strength and wisdom to rise in their own time, in their way. It's hard to watch someone you love struggle, to feel powerless in the face of their suffering.

But true love means allowing them the dignity of their own experiences. Your role isn't to rescue—it's to walk alongside them, to show compassion, and to encourage them to keep going. The most powerful gift you can offer is your unwavering belief in their ability to find their way, coupled with your inner stability and light. When you release the pressure of trying to save others, you free yourself from exhaustion and frustration, and you free them to grow in their strength. You shift from trying to control the uncontrollable to simply being present.

And in doing so, you become a source of inspiration, not a crutch. So, be kind. Be patient. Be understanding. But know that the greatest growth happens when we face our struggles head-on. Trust in their ability to rise, and in the meantime, nurture your own peace and balance. Because in the end, the most profound transformations come not from being saved, but from realizing that we have the power to save ourselves.

19

You know that feeling when a friend asks how you're doing, and instead of brushing it off with a generic "I'm fine," you choose to open up? You lower your walls and share how things have truly been

—how hard, overwhelming, or uncertain life has felt lately. And instead of dismissing your words or changing the subject, they listen. They hold space for you with genuine care and attention, making you feel seen, heard, and understood. That kind of friend changes everything. It's not about solving your problems or giving advice; it's about their presence—their willingness to sit with you in your truth without judgment.

They don't rush to fix things or gloss over your struggles. They simply let you be real. In doing so, they remind you that you're not alone. Friends like that are rare. They make life's burdens feel lighter, even if nothing else changes, simply by showing up with empathy and kindness. Their support feels like a soft place to land when the world feels unsteady. It's easy to underestimate the power of being truly heard. But in moments of vulnerability, it means everything. These are the friendships that remind our connection isn't about perfection or pretending to have it all together—it's about sharing the messy, human parts of ourselves and knowing someone is there to hold space for it all.

Only a narcissist could spend years professing to be your one true love, weaving an intricate web of deceit and manipulation, making you believe you're the center of their universe, and then suddenly, without warning or explanation, discard you like yesterday's trash, leaving you stunned, heartbroken, and bewildered. They'll erase you from their life like a pesky mistake, block your number, unfollow you on social media, and pretend you never existed, all while moving on to their next conquest, their next victim, their next source of supply.

But what's even more astonishing is their ability to convince themselves and others that you're the one who's crazy, that you're the one who's overreacting, that you're the one who's unworthy of love. They'll rewrite history, distort reality, and fabricate lies to justify their actions, leaving you to question your sanity and wonder if you ever truly knew them at all. But remember, their actions are not a reflection of your worth, but a testament to their emptiness, their lack of empathy, and their inability to truly love.

20

There is profound beauty in stillness and quiet grace in acceptance. In a world that constantly urges us to move, achieve, and chase, we often forget the power of simply being. Stillness is not emptiness—it is the fullness of presence. It is the space where clarity emerges, where the chaos within settles, and where we reconnect with ourselves. When we allow ourselves to pause, we discover a beauty that exists beyond the noise—a beauty found in the moment, in the breath, in the awareness of being alive.

Acceptance, too, holds its quiet strength. It is not resignation or defeat, but the wisdom to embrace life as it unfolds. When we stop resisting what is, we free ourselves from unnecessary suffering. Acceptance allows us to make peace with the present moment, even when it doesn't look like what we hoped for. It teaches us that growth often lies not in changing our circumstances but in changing how we see them. Stillness and acceptance go hand in hand, offering us a path to grace. In the stillness, we find ourselves; in acceptance, we find freedom. Together, they guide us to live more fully, more authentically, and with a deeper sense of gratitude.

21

"The most beautiful people we encounter in life are often those who have walked through fire." They've faced defeat, endured pain, struggled with hardship, and experienced loss in ways that most of us can scarcely comprehend. Yet, it is through these trials that their true beauty emerges—not the kind that can be seen on the surface, but the kind that radiates from deep within. These individuals have mastered the delicate art of resilience. They know what it's

Like to be broken, to feel lost, and to question everything they once believed. Despite the weight of their struggles, they rise again, emerging stronger and more empathetic. It is this journey through darkness that shapes their hearts with unparalleled sensitivity. Having experienced suffering, they possess an extraordinary capacity for compassion. Their beauty is not about how they look but about how they make others feel. It's a quiet yet powerful presence that brings warmth and healing.

They've learned to understand life on a deeper level, seeing the world not just with their eyes but with their hearts. Their understanding of human pain allows them to connect with others in a way that feels genuine, raw, and deeply comforting. They listen without judgment, offer support without expectation, and extend kindness without restraint. What makes these people so special is that they have walked through their own storms and emerged with an appreciation for life that many who haven't faced adversity might lack. It's a gentle strength that comes from understanding that everything is temporary and that every struggle holds a lesson.

Their hearts are filled with love—not only for those around them but for themselves—a love forged in the fire of their experiences. Beauty like this doesn't happen by chance. It is born from enduring the hardest parts of life and choosing, again and again, to move forward with an open heart. It's a choice to see the good, even when things seem impossible. The most beautiful people aren't simply lucky or gifted; they've faced the worst and found a way to rise above it, transforming their scars into strength and offering that strength to others.

So, when you encounter someone with this kind of beauty— someone whose spirit shines through their words and actions— remember that their light is born from their struggles. They've walked through the dark and emerged with a heart that knows love, kindness, and true compassion. That's a beauty that cannot be bought or imitated. It is earned, hard-won, and priceless.

22

Engaging in a deep, soul-stirring conversation with someone who possesses both a luminous mind and a kindred soul is a form of intimacy that defies the physical. It's an experience that reaches into the core of who you are, awakening something raw, tender, and transformative. It's a kind of connection that feels like making love without touch—one that nourishes your spirit, broadens your perspective, and leaves you feeling deeply seen, heard, and understood in ways words alone could never fully convey.

These exchanges go beyond the mere sharing of thoughts; they are a meeting of spirits, a merging of emotions and ideas stripped of masks and pretenses. Every question draws out a hidden truth, every shared vulnerability unravels another layer of your being, and every moment carries the unspoken promise that here, in this space, you are safe to exist as you are. Time seems to dissolve, the outside world fades, and what remains is the exquisite resonance of two souls aligned in perfect harmony.

When you encounter someone whose intellect challenges you and whose spirit embraces you, it's as if they hold a key to doors within yourself you didn't know existed. They awaken parts of you that have long been dormant, their insights urging you to think in new directions, their curiosity mirroring your own, and their warmth creating a sanctuary where you can share your dreams, doubts, and desires without fear.

In their presence, you find pieces of yourself you never thought someone else could recognize. These connections are rare in a world often content with shallow exchanges. They are love in its purest form—an intimacy born of shared curiosity, mutual respect, and the courage to be unapologetically yourself. There's no need for physical touch because the bond itself is an embrace—a quiet, unspoken merging that wraps you in the comfort of being truly understood. The imprint of such moments lingers long after the conversation ends.

Fragments replay in your mind, inspiring and soothing you, as though the dialogue has become a part of you. It changes you, reshaping how you see yourself and the world, leaving behind a quiet gratitude for having experienced something so rare and profound. When you find a connection like this, cherish it. These are the moments that remind us of what it truly means to connect—not just with another person, but with the truest parts of ourselves. Intimacy begins here, in the fearless exchange of authenticity, and it flourishes in the space built by shared respect and understanding. This is the kind of love that doesn't just touch you—it transforms you. Softly, deeply, and in ways you'll carry forever.

23

When connections are genuine, they exist beyond the confines of time and circumstance. They can be silenced by distance, disrupted by life's chaos, or buried beneath years of growth and change, but they are never truly broken. A bond that touches the soul isn't something fleeting—it's a presence, a quiet energy that lingers, waiting for the right moment to resurface. Revisit that person, that memory, that place where your spirit felt most alive, and you'll see: real connections defy the linearity of time.

They don't fade—they simply pause, like a song waiting to be played again. The laughter, the understanding, the shared rhythm of being—it all rushes back in an instant, filling the void of years as though no time had passed at all. In those moments, you're reminded that some ties are immune to the erosion of time and space. True connections are timeless. They may shift, evolve, or go dormant, but their essence is indelible. They reflect the deepest parts of ourselves, showing us who we were, who we are, and the unchanging truths that tether us to what's real and meaningful. They're a quiet reminder that the things meant for us, the people meant for us, don't vanish—they simply wait for their time to reemerge.

24

There are people who enter your life and quietly change everything. They see you in ways no one else ever has, touch parts of your soul you didn't even know existed, and make you feel understood in a world that rarely pauses to notice. But here's the catch: once they're gone, you'll never find anyone quite like them again.

In a world obsessed with speed and disposability, we've been taught to believe that everything—and everyone—is replaceable. Break it? Buy another. Lose someone? Move on. There's always something newer, better, waiting just around the corner—or so we're told. But the truth is, some people are once-in-a-lifetime. Their presence, their laughter, the way they make you feel at home—these are things you can never replicate, no matter how many new faces come into your life.

The tragedy is, that we often don't realize their value until it's too late. We hurt the people who mean the most to us—sometimes out of selfishness, sometimes out of pride, and sometimes simply because we think they'll always be there. We say things in anger, or worse, we say nothing at all, letting distance creep in like a shadow. We assume we'll have time to fix it, that they'll understand, that they'll wait.

But not everyone does. Some people walk away quietly. They carry their hurt without making a scene, leaving behind a silence that speaks louder than words ever could. And when they're gone, you'll feel it. The emptiness they leave behind is unlike any other. You'll search for them in others, hoping to find their magic in a new face, a new voice— but you won't. No one else will ever shine quite the same way they did. The hardest part? It's not just losing them—it's knowing that you could have done more.

That a careless word, a moment of neglect, or a failure to show gratitude pushed them away. Relationships are fragile, like the finest glass, and once broken, no amount of regret can make them whole again. So, be careful with the hearts you touch. Handle them with kindness and care, especially those who bring light into your life. Speak with intention, act with love, and never take them for granted. The rarest connections are also the most delicate. When they're gone, no substitute will ever fill the space they leave behind.

25

The most terrible loneliness is not the kind that comes from being alone, but the kind that comes from being misunderstood; the loneliness of standing in a crowded room, surrounded by people who do not see you, who do not hear you, who do not know the true essence of who you are. And in that loneliness, you feel as though you are fading, disappearing into the background until you are nothing more than a ghost, a shadow of your former self. It's that soul- deep ache of being surrounded by people—friends, family, colleagues—yet feeling completely invisible.

You may smile, nod, and go through the motions, but inside, you feel a sense of isolation that words can't fully capture. You feel as though no one truly gets you, as if the truest parts of you are hidden, left unrecognized, while the world only acknowledges the version of you that fits in. This kind of loneliness hits hard because it isn't about the absence of people; it's about the absence of connection. You crave to be seen for who you really are, to have someone understand your soul's language, your quirks, your dreams, and the complexities of your heart.

But when you're misunderstood, it feels as if there's an unbridgeable gap between your inner world and the outside one. It's like standing behind a glass wall, desperately hoping someone will look through and truly see you, only to realize they're gazing right past you. In that space of feeling unknown, you start to question yourself. You wonder if you should change, if you should become what the world expects or desires, just to feel a hint of acceptance. But even then, the loneliness doesn't vanish; it only grows. Because the deeper tragedy is the slow fading of your own essence, the of you that you start to hide or let go of, simply to belong.

You become a shadow, a ghost of the vibrant self you once were, drifting silently, holding onto the hope that one day, someone might understand. What makes this kind of loneliness so painful is that it's not just the longing to be loved—it's the longing to be known, and loved for being known. For someone to look at the parts of you that are messy, complicated, and even broken, and to say, "I see you. I understand.

And I'm here." It's the yearning for someone to hear your heart's quietest whispers and to feel the depths of your soul without judgment or expectation. Yet, even in that terrible loneliness, there's a quiet strength. There's resilience in holding onto your essence, even when it feels invisible. There's courage in keeping your light alive, in refusing to let the world's misunderstanding extinguish the fire within you.

You may feel unseen, but the truth is, your uniqueness, your complexity, is what makes you extraordinary. Somewhere, someone will value that. And until then, you can value that. Sometimes, the journey through being misunderstood leads to a deeper understanding of yourself. It teaches you to embrace who you are, even if the world isn't ready to. It invites you to find peace in your own company, to nurture the parts of yourself that feel lonely and unacknowledged. And, in time, you may discover that the right connections—the ones that see you, hear you, and know you—come when you least expect them.

So, hold on. Keep your essence alive. Refuse to become a shadow, even if that means standing alone for a while. Your true self deserves to be celebrated, and though the wait may feel long, the beauty of being fully known is worth every moment. Your people— the ones who truly understand your soul—are out there, and when they find you, the terrible loneliness will start to fade. You'll realize that your essence was never meant to be hidden. It was always meant to shine.

26

"You are so brave and quiet I forget you are suffering." You navigate life with such grace and resilience that many overlook the silent battles you face. They see your strength, your ability to keep showing up, and your calm demeanor—but not the weight you carry or the courage it takes just to keep moving forward. There is a profound beauty in the quiet strength you possess. It's not loud or attention- seeking but steady, enduring, and deeply inspiring.

In a world that often celebrates only the obvious victories, your silent perseverance is a reminder of what true bravery looks like. Every single day, you make the choice to rise again—to face your challenges, to care for others, to keep going despite the storms within. That choice is not just admirable—it's extraordinary. You may feel unseen or misunderstood, but your quiet courage leaves an indelible mark on those who truly notice.

Often, the strongest people are the ones who bear their struggles quietly, who don't show their scars, and yet still choose to radiate kindness and hope. You may think your efforts go unnoticed, but know this: your resilience and the light you bring to others make a difference. Even when it feels like no one sees the battle within, your strength inspires more than you realize. But remember—being strong doesn't mean you must bear it all alone.

True strength includes acknowledging when you need help and giving yourself permission to rest, to feel, and to heal. Asking for support is not a weakness; it's one of the bravest things you can do. If you ever feel invisible or as though your struggles are unnoticed, know this: there are people who see you, who are in awe of the quiet strength you carry, and who are deeply grateful for the hope and light you share. You are not alone, and your perseverance matters profoundly.

The world needs more people like you—those who lead with quiet bravery, with hearts full of compassion, and with an enduring commitment to keep moving forward, no matter the obstacles. You are extraordinary in ways words cannot fully fathom.

27

There's a quiet devastation in the spaces left by words unspoken and endings unexplained. It's not the departure itself that haunts us but the absence of acknowledgment— the silence stretching where closure should be. These unresolved moments carve deeply into us, leaving wounds that heal not with clarity but with time and self-reckoning. Yet, hidden within this ache lies a profound opportunity to reshape our understanding of loss and resilience. We are storytellers by nature, endlessly seeking meaning in the events of our lives.

When a relationship ends without explanation, it disrupts that narrative, leaving us scrambling to piece together fragments of what remains. We revisit conversations, scrutinize memories, and question our role in the unraveling. But what we're truly searching for is not merely answers—it's permission to move forward. Life, however, often denies us that luxury. Unfinished endings are a different kind of teacher. They strip away our illusions of control and force us into the uncharted terrain of uncertainty.

This is where transformation begins—not in the resolution we crave but in the resilience we cultivate in its absence. It's an uncomfortable truth: the closure we seek rarely comes from others. It is something we must create for ourselves. In this way, unspoken goodbyes mirror life itself: unpredictable, unresolved, and often devoid of the tidy conclusions we expect. They remind us of the limits of our influence over others and the need to anchor ourselves in something steadier—our inner peace.

To live is to experience loss, and to grow is to learn that not all losses come with explanations. But how do we navigate this ambiguity? How do we quiet the restless thoughts and unmet longings stirred by unanswered goodbyes? The answer lies not in seeking external resolution but in embracing the silence as a space for reflection and renewal. The discomfort of uncertainty can become a catalyst for self-discovery—a moment to ask not why someone left but what their absence teaches us about our own strength.

Philosophers and thinkers across time have grappled with the challenge of letting go. The Stoics taught us to focus not on what we cannot control but on what lies within our power: our perceptions, our responses, and our ability to grow. Marcus

Aurelius reminds us that tranquility is found not in external circumstances but in aligning our minds with the present moment. These teachings offer a roadmap through the fog of unspoken goodbyes, urging us to cultivate inner stability when external answers elude us.

Letting go of the need for closure doesn't mean forgetting or ignoring the pain. It means honoring the loss while choosing not to let it define us. It means shifting our focus from what we've lost to what remains and what we can build from here. This process is neither quick nor easy, but it is transformative. Over time, the unanswered questions lose their sting, and the silence becomes less of a void and more of a canvas—a space where we can create our own meaning. It's in these moments of growth that we discover something remarkable: the strength to stand unshaken in the face of life's uncertainties.

Every unanswered goodbye teaches us patience, grace, and the ability to carry on without the neat conclusions we once thought we needed. They show us that our worth is not defined by who stays or goes but by the courage we display in the aftermath. The pain of unresolved endings doesn't simply vanish. It lingers, reshaping us in subtle ways. But its presence is not just a reminder of loss—it's a testament to our capacity for love, hope, and vulnerability. And with time, the edges of that pain soften, giving way to a quiet strength that no unanswered question can diminish.

So, what does it mean to embrace the unknown? To let go of the demand for answers and instead find meaning within ourselves? Perhaps it's about trusting that we are more resilient than we believe—that we can face life's uncertainties with an open heart.

Perhaps it's about choosing to see each loss as an invitation to grow—a chance to step into the fullness of who we are, even when the path ahead feels unclear.

In the end, the silence left by an unspoken goodbye is not just an absence; it's a space brimming with potential. It's an opportunity to rewrite our story—not with answers but with the wisdom gained in their absence. And maybe, just maybe, the most profound closure is realizing we don't need closure at all.

28

At the end of the day, it's about the people who are by your side when life gets hard. It's about the people who are there when you need them the most. It's about the people who say "we've got this" when you are facing challenges. It's about the people who notice when you're not yourself. It's about the people who check in on you when you have been more quiet than usual. It's about the people you'd rather sit in comfortable silence with than make small talk with.

It's about the people who raise an eyebrow and know you're lying when you say you are okay when you're not. It's about the people who know your coffee order off by heart, and when you need one. It's about the people who text you to say they are thinking of you on the days that are difficult for you. Put simply, it's about the people who think of you. It's about the people who notice. It's about the people who show up in the smallest but most meaningful ways. It's about the people who stay, through it all.

29

"Tears of the Strong" Strong people wear their strength like armor, shielding the world from seeing their cracks. They carry the burdens of others, mend hearts that aren't theirs, and whisper words of hope even when their voices tremble. But when the night comes and the world grows quiet, their strength gives way to silence. It's in those moments, under the dim glow of the moon, that the weight becomes too much. They cry—not for weakness, but because their hearts need release.

They cry for the battles they've fought in silence. They cry for the pain they've endured without complaint. They cry because they've spent so much time holding others together, that they've forgotten how to heal themselves. The strongest people know the value of tears. They know that crying doesn't diminish their strength—it amplifies it. It's a reminder that they're human, that their struggles are real, and that even the strongest need to break sometimes to rebuild. These quiet tears are sacred.

They're the proof of resilience, the evidence of a soul brave enough to face its shadows. When morning comes, these same strong people will rise again, their hearts a little lighter, their spirits a little stronger, ready to face the world once more. So if you ever find yourself crying in the solitude of the night, remember this: you're not breaking. You're healing. And that, in itself, is strength.

30

"Taking advantage of someone who is kind to you is the lowest level of humanity!" Exploiting the kindness of others represents a profound moral failing, a descent to the lowest depths of human behavior. Kindness, a virtue freely given, is not a license for manipulation or self- serving actions. To take advantage of someone's generosity, trust, and goodwill is to betray the very essence of human decency. It's a violation of the unspoken contract of mutual respect that underpins healthy relationships, a demonstration of a profound lack of empathy and disregard for the well-being of others. Such actions not only inflict harm on the victim but also reveal a deep-seated moral corruption within the perpetrator

31

You didn't lose the love of your life; you broke free from the chains of a predator who drained your joy, strength, and identity. A narcissist isn't your soul mate—they're a master manipulator hiding behind a carefully crafted mask. The person you see at the end of the relationship, the one who discarded you without empathy, is who they've been all along. Their charm, their "magic," their love-bombing—all of it was a performance.

False promises and shallow words disguised their real agenda: to control, exploit, and feed off your emotional energy while breaking down your confidence. What you endured wasn't love— it was a calculated game of power. Gaslighting, criticism, and emotional manipulation weren't acts of affection but weapons used to keep you doubting yourself. Their betrayals weren't mistakes; they were deliberate moves to hold you captive in their cycle of abuse. But here's the powerful truth:

You didn't lose a family member—you escaped a nightmare. Walking away from that toxic cycle took unimaginable strength. Breaking free from someone who pretends to love but thrives on control isn't easy, but you did it. And now, you're standing in the light of freedom, no longer bound to their lies. Healing begins when you accept this: you weren't loved, you were used. But that does not define your worth or your future. You were created for real love, genuine connection, and a life filled with joy, authenticity, and peace.

God's love has always been there for you—constant, unwavering, and true. He sees you, knows you, and calls you His own. "The Lord is close to the brokenhearted and saves those who are crushed in spirit." – Psalm 34:18 You are worthy of being truly seen, deeply heard, and genuinely valued. Never settle for less than the love and respect you deserve. Real love isn't a game or manipulation—it's kind, patient, and true. As you heal, remember this: the best is yet to come. You've reclaimed your life, and the right people, the right love, and the right future are waiting for you.

32

Sometimes the bravest thing you can do is walk away. Walk away from those who diminish your worth, who thrive on control, or who drain your energy with their toxicity. Life is too short to stay entangled with narcissists who twist reality, bigots who refuse to see beyond their narrow world, or those who demand it's their way or no way. You don't owe anyone an explanation for prioritizing your peace.

Their chaos isn't your responsibility to fix, and their toxicity doesn't deserve a place in your heart. Surround yourself with people who lift you, who inspire growth, and who meet you with respect and kindness. Walking away isn't weakness; it's strength. It's a declaration that your mental health, self-respect, and happiness matter more than tolerating environments that crush your spirit. Choose peace. Choose yourself. And remember, leaving behind what weighs you down is the first step toward soaring higher.

33

One day, you'll realize that the same person cannot be found twice in life. Not everyone is replaceable. Be careful with the hearts you touch, and even more so with the ones you wound. In today's fast-moving world, we've become accustomed to thinking that everyone and everything is temporary. We glorify the idea of "moving on," believing there's always something better waiting just around the corner.

But some connections are once-in-a-lifetime. Their essence, their understanding, the way they made you feel seen and valued—these cannot be replicated, no matter how many new people you meet. Losing such a person isn't just losing a relationship; it's losing a piece of yourself that only they could bring to life. We often hurt the ones who matter most, sometimes unknowingly, sometimes out of our fears or pride. It's easy to forget the weight of our actions or the permanence of our words when caught in the heat of the moment.

We assume they'll always be there, that there will always be time to fix things. But the harsh reality is that time isn't always a healer, and second chances aren't guaranteed. The person you once hurt might be the one person who understood you best. And when they're gone, the emptiness they leave behind can be unbearable. Not everyone waits for apologies. Not everyone gives endless chances. Some people will walk away quietly, carrying their hurt with them, and you'll only realize what you lost when it's too late. You'll search for their presence in others, but no one else will shine quite the same.

Their laughter, their love, and their unique magic will remain unmatched. Be mindful of the way you treat those who mean the most to you. The careless moments—harsh words, neglect, or indifference— can create wounds that never fully heal. A single moment of thoughtlessness can sever a connection that took years to build. Relationships, like glass, can shatter when handled carelessly, and no amount of regret can restore them to their original form. Cherish those who bring light into your life.

Speak with kindness, act with intention, and show gratitude while they're still within reach. Love deeply and authentically, knowing that the rarest connections are also the most fragile. Once gone, they may never return, and no substitute will ever fill the space they leave behind. Be careful who you hurt. Some souls, some bonds, are irreplaceable.

34

I used to be that person who reaches out. I used to be that person who bridges people. I used to be that person who always wanted to talk things out. I used to be that person who patches things first before others. I used to be that person who sets up gatherings. I used to be that person who always wanted to be with my friends and be there for them. Yes, I used to be that person who prioritizes others. But sometimes, things happen and people change. Even me. Experiences taught me important lessons in life. I no longer feel the need to always be that person.

When people no longer value and see you as someone like they used to see you before, the best way to respond is to just stop. When people no longer care, it's okay to stop caring for them. It's okay to stop reaching out and just be within your space. It's okay to not bridge anymore especially when people no longer wanted to cross it. It's okay to be silent when people no longer want to talk it out. It's okay to stop patching things up when people have already decided not to. It's okay to prioritize yourself before others. Yes, It's okay to end friendships. As we navigate life's stormy seas, we all deserve the peace we need. And if ending some friendships helps, then be it.

35

In our darkest moments, we don't need solutions or advice. What we yearn for is simply human connection

—a quiet presence, a gentle touch. These small gestures are the anchors that hold us steady when life feels like too much. Please don't try to fix me. Don't take on my pain or push away my shadows. Just sit beside me as I work through my inner storms. Be the steady hand I can reach for as I find my way. My pain is mine to carry, my battles mine to face.

But your presence reminds me I'm not alone in this vast, sometimes frightening world. It's a quiet reminder that I am worthy of love, even when I feel broken. So, in those dark hours when I lose my way, will you just be here? Not as a rescuer, but as a companion. Hold my hand until the dawn arrives, helping me remember my strength. Your silent support is the most precious gift you can give. It's a love that helps me remember who I am, even when I forget.

36

A shadow is cast behind a shining person. Behind the splendor and bright smiles, there is a hidden darkness that, is difficult to notice.

37

At the beginning of any relationship, everything seems perfect. There are sweet gestures and endless efforts, and it feels like a dream. But as time goes by, you start to see the sides of people they didn't show before, their true nature, their priorities, and how they treat you. And that's not necessarily a bad thing! It's during these times that you realize whether they are worth keeping in your life or not.

Don't be blind to the truth. If someone shows you who they truly are, especially if they repeatedly do things that hurt you, believe them. Don't justify their behavior just because you want to hold on to the "perfect" person they were when you first met.

Remember, love isn't about finding someone perfect; it's about choosing someone whose imperfections you can live with. But there's a big difference between flaws and toxicity. If you're not respected, loved properly, and given the effort you deserve, it might be time to ask yourself: "Is this the person I want to spend my life with?"

Be brave enough to walk away if you need to. Sometimes, letting go is the most loving thing you can do for yourself. And don't be afraid to start over. As they say, the right one won't make you question your worth.

So here's a reminder for you: Love yourself enough to know when to stay and when to walk away. You deserve someone who will show you their true self and make you feel safe and loved, not worn out and tired.

Embrace the light within you, and let it guide you to the love you truly deserve.

38

The lack of respect was the closure, a boundary drawn in the sand.
The lack of empathy was the closure, a bridge burned, disconnecting hearts and hands.
The lack of trust was the closure, a shattered vase, impossible to mend.

The lack of apology was the closure, unspoken words, a heavy burden to amend.
The lack of appreciation was the closure, a flower unwatered, wilted and gray.

The lack of self-awareness was the closure, a mirror shattered, reflection lost along the way.
The lack of honesty was the closure, a veil of deceit, obscuring truth and light.

The lack of love was the closure, a flame extinguished, warmth, and comfort lost in the night.
The lack of care was the closure, a final goodbye, a door closed, a chapter ended.

39

Men, let me tell you what it means to truly understand a woman and align with her. If you've ever tried to box her in, calling her soft, gentle, or fragile, you've missed her essence. A woman is so much more than that. She's the storm that shakes the silence and the tide that pulls you in before you even realize it. She is chaos wrapped in grace, a force of nature you cannot control. And without her, you do not survive. She is Kali, the protector who destroys what no longer serves. She stands for truth, cutting through illusions and bringing light to the darkest places.

To align with her, you must respect her fire and allow it to transform you. She is Apsara, a vision of beauty and joy. She moves through life with elegance, reminding you of the magic in every moment. To align with her, celebrate her, and cherish the light she brings into your life. She is Shakti, the energy that creates and sustains life. She is the power behind all growth and change. To align with her, honor her strength, and understand that her power is not here to compete with yours—it is here to uplift both of you. A woman's emotions are her way of speaking. Her tears, her anger, her joy—they all have meaning. They are not weaknesses; they are her truth. To align with her, listen deeply and let her know she is safe to express herself with you. She needs to feel safe, not just physically, but emotionally. She wants to know that she can be her full self—her dreams, her fears, her vulnerabilities—without judgment. When you create that safety, she will trust you completely. Her chaos is not something to fear. It is the energy that clears the way for something new to grow. Instead of trying to control it, learn to move with it. Trust that her storms bring clarity and purpose.

A woman craves connection. She doesn't just want your presence; she wants to feel understood. She wants your soul to meet hers. To align with her, let your walls down and meet her with honesty and vulnerability. She is a mirror, reflecting your truth back to you. In her presence, you'll see the parts of yourself you've hidden. When you align with her, you grow not just as a partner, but as a person. She is not here to be controlled or fixed. She is not your rival or your equal in sameness.

She is your complement, your balance. To align with her is to recognize her as your partner in every sense— someone who strengthens you as you strengthen her. So dear man, Aligning with her starts with aligning with yourself. Let go of the need to control, and instead, surrender to her flow. She is not here to complete you; she is here to awaken you. When you truly align with her, you will realize she is life itself. She is its rhythm, its pulse, its heart. And when you honor her, you honor all of creation.

40

The meaning of true love from a man. I hate to say this but most women will go their entire lifetime and never experience the meaning of actual true love. It's even slightly depressing to think that most people will never understand how powerful this picture is. This gentleman is a prime example of how men should be treating their partner with every day that passes. We unfortunately live in a generation with men who have no idea what it takes to be a real man. Let me give you a couple of examples of a real man ...... A real man asks about your day and genuinely cares about the answer.

A real man respects your boundaries and never forces you to do anything you're not ready to do. He makes time for you and takes that time to learn and understand who you are as a person. A real man consistently shows you the definition of effort with every day that passes. He will call you randomly throughout the day just to check on you and your mental health. A real man is undeniably committed to you and looks for new ways to fall in love with you with every day that passes. He makes protecting your heart a number one priority. A real man never makes permanent decisions based on temporary emotions. He never confuses you about where you stand in his life.

A real man apologizes when he is wrong and stays true to his character. He doesn't mind hurting other people's feelings to protect yours. A real man gives you affection without sexual expectation. A real man refuses to entertain any woman who isn't you. He has genuine intentions with you from day one and shows you how it truly feels to be a priority rather than an option. A real man will help you heal from the trauma that nobody apologized for. A real man values you and would never put themselves in a position to lose you. Take my advice and wait for the man that never let's you fall asleep at night questioning your self-worth.

41

Don't let anyone invalidate or minimize how you feel. If you feel something, you feel it and it's real to you. Nothing anyone says has the power to invalidate that, ever. No one else sees life through your eyes. No one else has lived through your experiences. And so, no one else has the right to dictate or judge how you feel. Your feelings are important and you deserve to be heard. They are inherently valid and they matter. Don't let anyone make you believe otherwise.

You are allowed to be upset when someone hurts you. You are not obligated to always take on the role of the "bigger person" and invalidate your feelings. There is no need to immediately search for the lesson in the hurt, or thank the one who hurt you for gifting you resiliency. You are allowed to just feel hurt. Betrayed. Wounded. You don't have to swallow the pain. You don't have to let it simmer within you, only to bubble up when you least expect it.

The feelings of those who hurt you are not more important than your own. You don't owe them forgiveness. You don't owe them grace. You don't owe them understanding. You owe yourself all of that. You owe yourself the freedom to honor your feelings, however heavy they may be. Standing up for yourself doesn't make you argumentative. Sharing your feelings doesn't make you over-sensitive. And saying no doesn't make you uncaring or selfish. If someone doesn't respect your feelings, needs, and boundaries, the problem isn't you; it's them.

42

Life has already tested me enough, and I've learned that peace is priceless. I no longer have the patience for situations that drain my energy, disrupt my balance, or pull me into negativity. I crave environments that nourish my soul, people who bring warmth instead of chaos, and moments that feel like deep breaths instead of battles. If it doesn't align with my need for calmness and gentleness, I simply don't have the space for it. My well-being comes first, and I refuse to compromise it for anything or anyone.

43

I fought for it countless times before I finally let go. I tried to understand everything— over and over— even when it made no sense until I could no longer hold on. Perhaps, after all the struggles, my heart simply grew tired of waiting. Then one day, I woke up and realized that I, too, deserve to be understood, to be fought for, and to be loved.

44

So many people are suffering in relationships today because they refuse to let go of someone who isn't right for them: They know, deep down, that the relationship isn't working, but they hold on, believing they can change the other person. They convince themselves that if they just try harder, sacrifice more, or love enough, the person will finally "love them back" the way they deserve. The hardest part is realizing that no matter how much effort they put in, the other person has no intention of changing.

They remain stuck, pouring their energy into a relationship that only brings them pain. If you're in a relationship where the person is causing you more grief than happiness, it's time to let go. Accepting that things aren't working is the first and most important step to protecting yourself from further hurt. It's crucial to be honest with yourself and admit when à relationship is broken beyond repair. So many people suffer because they refuse to face the reality of their situation, hoping things will magically get better. But hope alone cannot fix a relationship.

If your current relationship isn't working, don't force it. The more you try to hold on to something that isn't meant to be, the more you'll hurt yourself in the process. Remember this: nobody can take your happiness away unless you allow it. Your happiness is your responsibilities in your hands, not someone else's. If you don't want others to mistreat you, you have the power to stop them. You deserve respect, love, and kindness, and if those things are no longer being served, it's time to walk away.

46

Perhaps one of the hardest things in the world is discovering the true face hidden behind the mask of someone you hold dear—and being unable to accept it. Knowing everything yet pretending to know nothing. After immense pain, betrayal, and broken trust, not everyone can scream in anger, cry their eyes out, or forgive generously. Nor does everyone possess the extraordinary strength to seek revenge. Some are left with a vague, intense sense of hurt—silent, unspoken, and deeply personal. A cold, bloodless battle fought within oneself. In this battle, one must endure countless sleepless nights of unbearable agony.

There are moments when one feels unbearable even to oneself, exhausted from trying to convince their own heart. The cruel stabs of shattered trust gnaw at the mind. And when you try to walk away from the relationship, stepping over the shards of broken trust to find peace, they shift the entire blame onto you. Their eyes show no remorse. They treat you as if you are the betrayer. But they never understand the struggle of walking away from a heart where, at one time, you sought refuge in God's name. They can't comprehend the mental agony, the powerless days, the pain of sleepless nights, the fire in your tear-dried eyes, or the silent screams tearing through your chest.

They don't realize how a lively person—once someone who tried to spread joy in everyone's life—becomes an empty shell, alive yet lifeless. They don't understand, nor do they want to. Sometimes, you feel like collapsing into someone's arms and crying your heart out. You long to share your deepest wounds, to find a bit of solace. You yearn for someone to comfort you with oceans of affection, caress your head, and soothe the blazing fire in your heart with tender love. You wish for your sleepless eyelids to finally find rest in a blissful slumber. Yet, like a fallen star, we never meet those things again—not the stories, not the love, not the relationships, nor the people. All that remains are sighs and an endless emptiness, scattered like fragrant autumn flowers along the path of life.

47

This is now my era of setting boundaries. I am finally removing myself from situations where I feel like I am not valued or treated well. I am now walking away from people who bring chaos into my mind or anyone who causes me too much pain. I am creating a borderline between me and those who only give me emotional distress. I am also setting boundaries for being so kind or considerate to people.

I am so sick of being taken for granted. I am so exhausted from the abuse that I receive from people who keep hurting me or letting me down over and over again just because they know that I am very forgiving. This is my era of respecting myself and focusing on my well-being. I've already had enough of people treating me poorly and taking advantage of the kindness that I offer them genuinely.

I am done believing that if I plant love, kindness, and compassion in people, it will also yield good results, and they will grow the same as what I planted. But I've seen so many ungrateful people, and I refuse to spend my life tolerating or dealing with the things I don't deserve. I am no longer allowing toxic and unkind people to have access to my life, and I believe that this is a simple act of prioritizing self-care. Unapologetically, I am now choosing to be kinder to myself.

48

I'm better this way, alone but safe. I don't fear getting hurt or someone leaving me. I have come out of that phase now, and I'm happy that I did. Many people are still there, but not me, not anymore. I'm good here, happy with my things, my choices, my favorites. I don't have to worry about anyone else's favorite or choice. Nobody controls my life here, nor do I try to control or change it for someone else.

I have no pressure to figure things out for them. Everybody has their life, so they should take their responsibility. Why do they wish or expect someone else to do things because they want? They should do it themselves. Just like I'm doing everything myself. I cook my food, I bring myself a coffee, and I set up a cozy and beautiful corner just to sit there and do my favorite things like reading, painting, or writing.

Or sometimes I just stay there, doing nothing. And there is no one to get bothered by this. I've come beyond the expectations. This feeling of living with freedom is something else; no love can provide it except self-love. I'm starting with it by accepting my habits and expecting no one to accept them. I'm better this way.

49

Evil isn't always a shadow lurking in the corner or a stranger with malicious intent. Often, it wears a familiar face—a smile you've trusted, a voice you've confided in, or someone you never thought capable of harm. It's the friend who betrays you, the loved one who manipulates you, or the person who uses your love and loyalty as weapons against you. Evil doesn't always shout; sometimes it whispers, sugarcoating its intentions, leaving you doubting your own judgment.

It hides behind charm, affection, or authority, making it harder to recognize until the damage is done. It prioritizes control, deceit, and power over genuine care. It creates confusion, leaving you questioning whether you're the problem when, in reality, it's their actions that drain your peace and happiness. They may seem loving in public but reveal their cruelty in private.

This duality can be devastating, leaving wounds that cut deep into your soul. But remember, just because evil is familiar doesn't mean you have to accept it. Familiarity should never be mistaken for safety. Trust your instincts. If something feels wrong, it probably is. It's not weakness to walk away; it's strength. Protect your heart, protect your peace, even if it means stepping away from people you once held close.

The hardest battles are the ones fought against those we care about. But your well-being, dignity, and worth are non-negotiable. You are not obligated to endure cruelty disguised as love. Let go of the familiar that harms you and make room for the peace and love you truly deserve.

50

Choose a man you can trust because trust will help you reach your full potential. A woman thrives when she has the right masculine energy in her life—a presence that brings security, support, and emotional stability. When she can work freely without fear, doubt, or unnecessary burdens, she steps into her highest self. But for this to happen, she must be with a man she can trust. Trust is the foundation of every meaningful relationship. When you have a partner you can rely on, it becomes easier to navigate life's challenges. You feel safe enough to be vulnerable, to dream bigger, and to embrace your femininity fully.

However, not every man is trustworthy. Sometimes, you may find yourself with a partner your soul refuses to trust—no matter how much you want to. This is a sign that something is not right. A woman's intuition is powerful. If your heart feels unsettled, if your body hesitates to relax in his presence, or if your mind constantly questions his words and actions, listen to those signals. Love should not be a battlefield of doubt. It should be a sanctuary where you feel seen, heard, and protected. Choosing the wrong man can drain your energy, make you second-guess yourself, and force you into survival mode rather than allowing you to flourish. At the core of a healthy relationship is a man who understands the weight of his masculine energy.

He doesn't dominate or control; instead, he provides a space where you can be yourself without fear. His strength does not lie in how loud he is but in how dependable, kind, and grounded he remains in all situations. A man who values your trust will never make you beg for reassurance—his actions will naturally provide it. If you find yourself unable to trust the person beside you, ask yourself why. Is it because of his actions? Is it because of unresolved wounds from your past? Or is it because something within you knows he is not meant to walk this journey with you? The most precious gift you can give yourself is discernment—

the ability to choose a man who aligns with your spirit, not just your emotions or circumstances.

Many women stay in relationships out of fear—fear of being alone, fear of judgment, or fear of starting over. But settling for a man you cannot trust will only lead to deeper wounds. Trust is not something you can force; it is something that must be felt and built over time. When a woman trusts her man, she can relax into her divine feminine nature. She doesn't have to be in constant defense mode, guarding her heart against betrayal. Instead, she can love freely, create fearlessly, and live abundantly.

Masculine energy matters in a woman's life. It is not about control but about balance. When a woman is with a man who truly embodies trustworthiness, she can work, create, and grow without emotional burdens weighing her down. She knows she has a solid foundation to return to at the end of the day. This allows her to be both soft and strong, nurturing yet ambitious. If you struggle to understand why trust feels so difficult for you, seeking therapy can be a powerful step.

A good therapist can help you unpack past wounds, recognize patterns, and guide you toward healthier relationship choices. Healing is not just about letting go of pain; it's about learning how to choose better for yourself moving forward. You deserve a man who makes you feel safe, not just physically but emotionally and spiritually. You deserve a partner who doesn't make you question your worth or his intentions. You deserve a relationship where trust is not a privilege but a natural foundation. At the end of the day, love should not feel like a gamble. Choose a man you can trust, and you will find yourself stepping into a life where you are loved, protected, and free to shine in your fullest power.

51

A woman is so dangerous when she bounces back after being hurt so badly. You can hurt a woman over and over again. You can break her heart, ruin her peace of mind, and even make her soul weep. You can leave a woman with a shattered heart and a damaged soul. But she can be a dangerous woman when she comes back. After surviving a battle that almost took her sanity away, she will become a different person. You can hurt a woman so badly that she will fall to her knees, begging for the universe to take away her pain.

You can leave her on the edge of giving up on herself. But when she learns to pick herself up, it will be too late for you to realize that you hurt the wrong person. A woman can be vulnerable, but she can also be resilient. She can be very forgiving, but she can also have no mercy after going through the worst things in life. So be careful with the woman that you choose to hurt because you might create a dangerous woman one day. REMEMBER NO WOMAN GOES TO A MAN WITH BAD INTENTIONS, A WOMAN IS A REFLECTION OF HOW SHE is..

52

Become so silent that those people never hear your voice or see your shadow again. Become invisible to them. Make a promise to yourself that you will never look back. If you keep this promise, you won't feel pain. This silence may choke you with unspoken cries, but it will leave the other person with regret. The truth is, we protest with words because we fear losing. But do you know something? The ones who never valued you as a person, the ones who made you feel suffocated with grief—they were never truly yours. So, live for yourself, love yourself. You have a Creator. Tell Him all your sorrows, pains, desires, and hopes. He will take care of everything.

Become so silent that those people never hear your voice or see your shadow again. Become invisible to them. Make a promise to yourself that you will never look back. If you keep this promise, you won't feel pain. This silence may choke you with unspoken cries, but it will leave the other person with regret. The truth is, we protest with words because we fear losing. But do you know something? The ones who never valued you as a person, the ones who made you feel suffocated with grief—they were never truly yours. So, live for yourself, love yourself. You have a Creator. Tell Him all your sorrows, pains, desires, and hopes. He will take care of everything.

53

The Ones Who Let Us Go

Do you ever wonder why some people seem so careless with us? As if they never hold on tightly, no matter how much we give or how deeply we love? It's painful to realize that some people don't fear losing us—not because we're not enough, but because they never truly planned on keeping us in the first place.

Life can be like that. We invest so much of ourselves in people who treat us like passing moments, while we see them as forever. It's lonely, isn't it? Watching them slip away as if we never mattered, leaving behind unanswered questions and a heart too heavy to carry alone. Maybe life is teaching us something through this —something about value, about our worth. It's a hard lesson, but perhaps it's a reminder that we should never beg to stay where we are not cherished.

55

Your suffering is never caused by the person you're blaming." Blame is an easy escape, but it never leads to freedom and encases you in a prison of false perception. It's tempting to believe that suffering is caused by someone else—that their words, their actions, or their choices are the reason for the pain. But what if the real source of suffering isn't what they did, but the way it is perceived, processed, and held onto? The mind has a way of creating narratives. It builds stories around pain, assigning fault and attaching emotions to past wounds. But the moment blame is given away, power is also given away.

Blame keeps the focus outward, waiting for someone else to change, apologize, or make things right. But what if peace doesn't depend on their actions? What if it has always been an internal choice? No one can control how others act. People will make mistakes, they will be unfair, and they will disappoint. But what happens next—the response, the emotions carried forward, the way the situation is interpreted—is entirely within personal control. And this is where true strength lies: in realizing that suffering isn't created by the external, but by the attachment to what cannot be changed.

Personal accountability is not about excusing others—it's about reclaiming power. It's the understanding that while pain is real, suffering is optional. It's the choice to see difficult situations as lessons instead of burdens, to shift perspective from victimhood to growth. The world will not always be kind, but inner peace is not determined by external forces.

Letting go of blame is not about denying hurt; it's about refusing to let it define the future. When responsibility is taken for thoughts, reactions, and emotions, life no longer feels like something that happens to you, but something shaped by you. Freedom begins the moment responsibility is claimed. The choice is always there: to remain bound by blame or to step forward in strength. In the end, the only true control is over oneself, and that is where real peace is found.

Betrayal doesn't come from enemies,it comes from those we trust, those we love, those we never thought capable of hurting us. It's a knife that cuts deep, not just through the skin but through the heart, through the soul. And the worst part? It's not the act itself but the realization that the person you once held dear was willing to let you break. You replay the moments in your head, wondering if there were signs you missed. Were their smiles ever real? Did their words ever hold truth? You question everything, including yourself. How could you have been so blind? How could they have been so cruel?

But here's what betrayal doesn't do: it doesn't end you. It breaks something inside, yes, but in that breaking, you find yourself. You learn that your heart still beats, even with the weight of disappointment. You discover that your worth was never in their hands to begin with. So, cry if you need to. Scream if you must. But don't stay in the pain they left you with. Stand up, walk away, and remember...betrayal is not the end of your story. It's just the part where you learn who truly deserves to be in the next chapter.

56

Some people are so worthy of admiration, not because of their appearance or their status but because of their resilience. They have experienced things that other people would never even have to bear witness to. They have weathered the hardiest Winters and still shine like the sun. They call on their worst experiences to advice and guide others from out of the dark.

Their patience knows no bounds and they are happy to walk beside others to guide them through the storm. When you're around these people you feel safe and seen. They know when you're struggling without you needing to utter a word, and their presence alone is uplifting. Cherish these people for they are the ones who have saved themselves, and make it their mission to save others. They are the light we need when the world feels dark. They are the inspiration that we are all seeking..

57

There are some people that are so worthy of admiration, not because of their appearance or their status but because of their resilience. They have experienced things that other people would never even have to bear witness to. They have weathered the hardiest Winters and still shine like the sun. They call on their worst experiences to advice and guide others from out of the dark. Their patience knows no bounds and they are happy to walk beside others to guide them through the storm. When you're around these people you feel safe and seen. They know when you're struggling without you needing to utter a word, and their presence alone is uplifting. Cherish these people for they are the ones who have saved themselves, and make it their mission to save others. They are the light we need when the world feels dark. They are the inspiration that we are all seeking.

The right man will look at you like you're the most precious thing he's ever seen, and in his eyes, you'll see a reflection of the love you've been waiting for. He'll honor your boundaries, protect your heart, and pour into you in ways that leave you overflowing. His love will be the kind that doesn't just make you feel safe—it makes you feel limitless.

58

With him, love won't just be an emotion—it will be an experience. His presence will feel like the softest embrace, his voice like a melody you never want to stop hearing. Every kiss will feel like the world has paused, every touch a reminder that you're exactly where you're meant to be. Trust the timing. It's divine. The love you're waiting for isn't late; it's being perfected. When he comes into your life, you'll understand why it couldn't have been anyone else. He'll show you what it means to be truly seen, fully known, and unconditionally loved.

With him, you'll feel like the most beautiful version of yourself because his love will bring out the best in you. When he arrives, he'll bring more than love—he'll bring magic. He'll hold your hand not just through the easy moments but through the storms, and with him, every trial will feel lighter because you'll face them together. His love will be your anchor and your wings, keeping you grounded while helping you soar. So, dear woman, don't settle. Wait for the man who sees your worth before you even speak a word. Wait for the one who will cherish your soul, adore your spirit, and love you in ways you've only dreamed of. The right man won't just be your partner—he'll be your forever. And when he arrives, you'll know that every second of the wait was worth it, because with him, love will finally feel like coming home.

59

No matter who you are, someone will misunderstand you. Someone will misjudge your heart, question your intentions, and see you through the lens of their insecurities, experiences, and assumptions. To one person, you'll be inspiring; to another, you'll be irritating. To some, your energy will be overwhelming; to others, it will be a source of comfort. The same actions that make one person love you will make another uncomfortable. The same words that heal one will offend another. This is the nature of perception— flawed, personal, and ever-changing. You will never be universally loved, or universally disliked.

No matter how much you adjust, shrink, or try to control the narrative, the world will see you as it wants to, not necessarily as you are. So why waste your life trying to mold yourself into something that pleases everyone? Why sacrifice authenticity for approval that will never be consistent? The truth is, you were not meant to be easily defined. You are complex, layered, and ever-evolving. The world will project its fears and desires onto you, but that is not your burden to carry. What is within your power is choosing to live in a way that feels real, raw, and right to you.

Because in the end, the loudest voice shaping your life should not be theirs—it should be your own. So, if the world will never agree on who you are… why not be the version of yourself that makes you feel most alive?

In the end, I chose to build a wall around my once- fragile heart—not to forget, but to safeguard the pieces of myself that remain unbroken. Brick by brick, I stacked my wounds, my lessons, my silent sorrows.

Every crack in the wall holds a story I no longer wish to carry. Yet, if one day a patient hand knocks—not to shatter, but to understand—perhaps this wall will begin to crumble. And slowly, I will learn to open my heart once more, not with fear, but with hope.

The Author

Sylvia Villalobos is a poet, storyteller, and seeker of life's hidden beauty. With an innate passion for weaving words into heartfelt expressions, Sylvia has spent years exploring themes of healing, self-discovery, and resilience.

Her journey toward wholeness has shaped not only her writing but also her outlook on life, inspiring others to embrace their imperfections and find strength in their vulnerability.

When she is not writing, Sylvia finds solace in her kitchen, where cooking becomes an artful meditation. Her love for food reflects her love for connection—to culture, to family, and the present moment. She also enjoys playing golf, a sport that offers her both challenge and relaxation, and she deeply appreciates the arts, finding inspiration in their many forms. Beyond the written page, she is an ardent appreciator of the world's wonders, whether in the stillness of nature or the vibrant energy of a bustling city.

"Fragments to Wholeness: A Journey Back to Self" is Sylvia's heartfelt offering to readers, an invitation to walk alongside her as she reflects on the challenges and triumphs of reclaiming her sense of self. Through poetry and prose, she invites you to discover your own journey toward healing and wholeness.